To the healing hands of Dr. Peter Newton

A las manos sanadoras del Dr. Peter Newton

Originally published in English as *We've Got the Whole World in Our Hands.* • Adapted from the song "He's Got the Whole World in His Hands." • Copyright © 2018 by Rafael López • Translated by Juan Pablo Lombana • Translation copyright © 2018 by Scholastic Inc. • All rights reserved. Published by Orchard Books and Scholastic en español imprints of Scholastic Inc., *Publishers since 1920.* ORCHARD BOOKS and design are registered trademarks of Watts Publishing Group, Ltd., used under license. SCHOLASTIC, SCHOLASTIC EN ESPAÑOL, and associated logos are trademarks and/or registered trademarks of Scholastic Inc. • The publisher does not have any control over and does not assume any responsibility for author or third-party websites or their content. • No part of this publication may be reproduced, stored in a retrieval system, or transmitted in any form or by any means, electronic, mechanical, photocopying, recording, or otherwise, without written permission of the publisher. For information regarding permission, write to Scholastic Inc., Attention: Permissions Department, 557 Broadway, New York, NY 10012. • This book is a work of fiction. Names, characters, places, and incidents are either the product of the author's imagination or are used fictitiously, and any resemblance to actual persons, living or dead, business establishments, events, or locales is entirely coincidental. • Library of Congress Cataloging-in-Publication Data available • ISBN 978-1-338-29950-2
10 9 8 7 6 5 4 3   21 22 23 24 25 • Printed in China   38 • This edition first printing, October 2018 • Book design by Rafael López and Patti Ann Harris

We've Got the Whole World in Our Hands

Tenemos el Mundo Entero en las Manos

RAFAEL LÓPEZ

ORCHARD BOOKS • NEW YORK

scholastic inc.

We've got the whole world in our hands.
We've got the whole world in our hands.

Tenemos el mundo entero en las manos.
Tenemos el mundo entero en las manos.

We've got you and you've got me in our hands!
We've got the whole world in our hands.

¡Te tenemos a ti y tú me tienes a mí en las manos!
Tenemos el mundo entero en las manos.

We've got the sun and the rain in our hands.
Tenemos el sol y la lluvia en las manos.

We've got the moon and the stars in our hands.
Tenemos la luna y las estrellas en las manos.

We've got the whole world in our hands.

Tenemos el mundo entero en las manos.

We've got the wind and the clouds in our hands!
We've got the whole world in our hands.

¡Tenemos el viento y las nubes en las manos!
Tenemos el mundo entero en las manos.

We've got the rivers and the mountains in our hands.

Tenemos los ríos y las montañas en las manos.

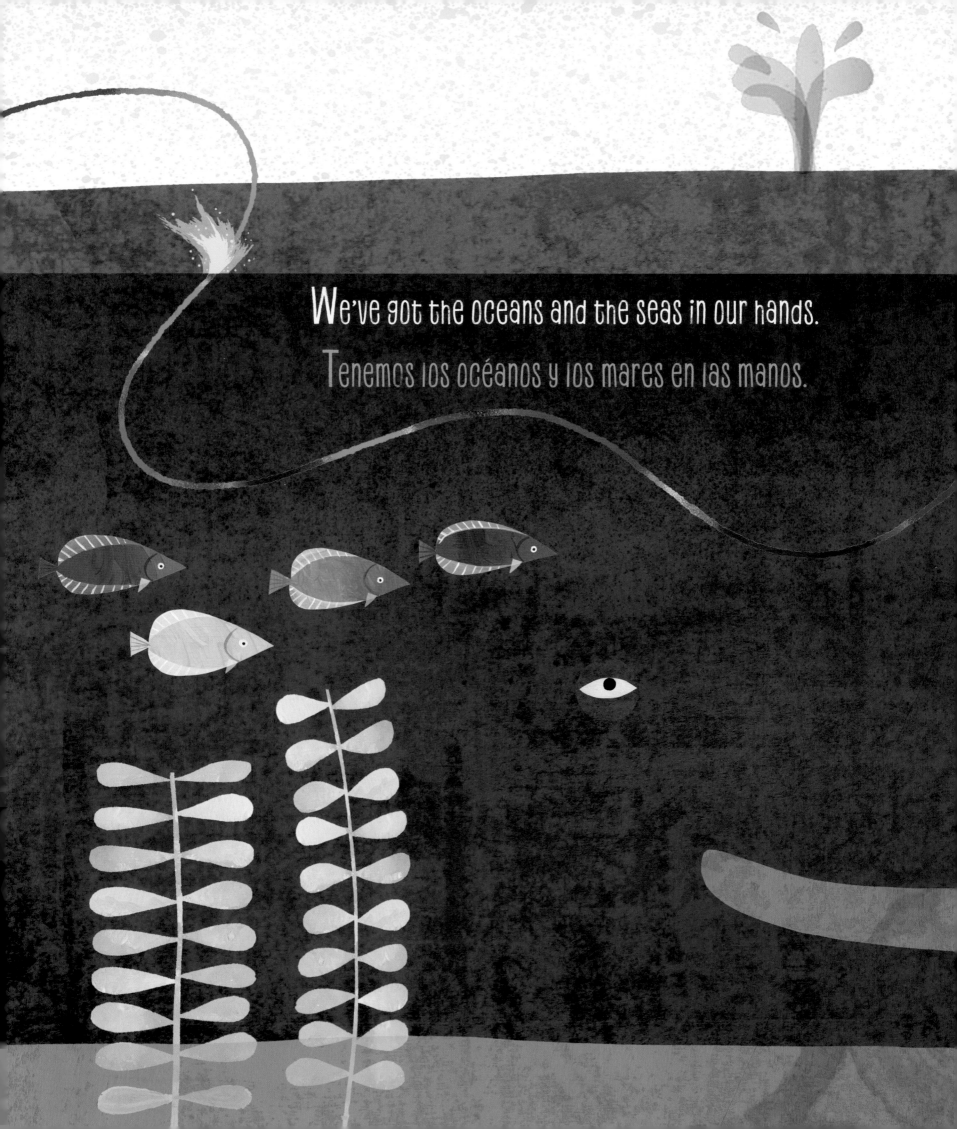

We've got the oceans and the seas in our hands.
Tenemos los océanos y los mares en las manos.

We've got you and you've got me in our hands.

Te tenemos a ti y tú me tienes a mí en las manos.

We've got the whole world in our hands.
Tenemos el mundo entero en las manos.

We've got everybody here in our hands.

Tenemos a todas las personas en las manos.

We've got the whole world in our hands.

Tenemos el mundo entero en las manos.

We've got everybody everywhere
in our hands.

Tenemos a todos los seres de todos
los lugares en las manos.

Tenemos el mundo entero en las manos.

We've got the whole world in our hands.

We've got the whole world
in our hands.

Tenemos el mundo
entero en las manos.

We've got the whole world in our hands
Tenemos el mundo entero en las manos

About "He's Got the Whole World in His Hands"

The origin of "He's Got the Whole World in His Hands" is uncertain, but this well-known spiritual has brought joy and hope to people around the world. The song was first published in a hymnal in 1927. Since that time, it has been rearranged and sung by many celebrated artists, including Marian Anderson, Mahalia Jackson, Laurie London, Reverend F.W. McGee, Odetta, and Nina Simone. The verses have been modified, but the message of unity has prevailed.

The Artist's Inspiration

Rafael López loves color because it speaks all languages. He uses an array of hues that come in large recycled salsa jars from Mexico, along with mixed media. Using his collection of tools and twigs, he scratches texture on the illustrated surface of wooden boards and watercolor paper. With his favorite pair of scissors, he cuts shapes out of Bristol paper and then plays with pen and ink, watercolor, and Adobe Photoshop to conjure the personalities of clouds and characters.

Acerca de "Tenemos el mundo entero en las manos"

Se desconoce el origen de "He's Got the Whole World in His Hands", pero este reconocido *spiritual* ha ofrecido alegría y esperanza a gente de todo el mundo. La canción se publicó por primera vez en 1927, en un himnario. Desde entonces, ha sido arreglada y cantada por muchos músicos reconocidos, como Marian Anderson, Mahalia Jackson, Laurie London, Reverend F.W. McGee, Odetta y Nina Simone. Los versos han sido modificados, pero el mensaje de unidad ha prevalecido.

La inspiración del artista

A Rafael López le encanta el color porque el color habla todos los idiomas. Usa una gran gama de colores que le llegan de México en grandes frascos de salsa reciclados y, también, una técnica mixta. Empleando su colección de herramientas y varas, Rafael crea texturas en las ilustraciones que ha hecho en superficies de tablas de madera o papeles para acuarelas. Con su par de tijeras favoritas corta papel Bristol y entonces juega con estilógrafos y tinta, acuarelas y Adobe Photoshop para darles vida y características a las nubes y los personajes.